HIDDEN NOTES
AND HIGH SEAS

ALICE, AN ADVENTIST GIRL

~ BOOK TWO ~

SANDY ZAUGG

Pacific Press® Publishing Association
Nampa, Idaho
Oshawa, Ontario, Canada
www.pacificpress.com

Edited by Elizabeth Lechleitner
Designed by Dennis Ferree
Cover and inside illustrations by Matthew Archambault
Research for cover illustration provided by
Judy M. Johnson

Additional copies of this book are available by
calling toll free 1-800-765-6955
or visiting http://www.adventistbookcenter.com

Library of Congress Cataloging-in-Publication Data

Zaugg, Sandra L., 1938-
Hidden notes and high seas / Sandy Zaugg.
p. cm. — (Alice, an Adventist girl; bk. 2)
Summary: While journeying to China so that her parents can
begin their missionary work, Alice joins a pair of red headed
twins in following mysterious messages around the ship,
weathering a storm, and observing the Sabbath.
ISBN: 0-8163-2052-7
[1.Ocean travel. 2. Twins. 3. Seventh-day Adventists.
4. Missionaries.] I. Title.

PZ7.Z2675Hi 2005
dc22   2004057287

05 06 07 08 09 • 5 4 3 2 1

Dedication

To the memory of my mother,
Irene Leach, who talked to me about
being a child in the 1920s and about
her experiences as a young adult
onboard ship—sz

Contents

1. Aboard the SS *President Jefferson* 7

2. "And Be Ye Alice?" 17

3. Pete and Andy and the Sabbath 24

4. A Storm at Sea 37

5. Where's Johnny? 45

6. A Little Homesickness 54

7. Saying Goodbye Again 61

8. Large Wall, Small Door 71

9. A Strange New World 83

CHAPTER 1

Aboard the SS *President Jefferson*

Mother sighed. "Well, I guess we're definitely on our way to China. No turning back now." She stood up straight and put her shoulders back. "Come on, Alice. Let's explore this ship."

Alice Stewart looked around. People were walking two by two along the deck. She saw Daddy lying in a big deck chair with Johnny asleep on his chest. Alice noticed that many deck chairs had long seats. They stuck way out in front, so people had to put their feet up when they sat in the chairs.

Mother reached for Alice's hand. They took a stairway to the deck above. She watched a group of men playing a strange game. They threw big rings made out of rope toward a post. The men were laughing and having fun.

"Mother," Alice said, as they started down a stairway on the other side of the deck, "how come there aren't any kids? I thought there'd be somebody to play with."

"There are some children staying in the cabin next to ours," Mother replied. "I saw them going in when we left to go up on deck. Two boys . . . just about your age, I think."

"Oh, look!" Alice said, peeking into a quiet room with tables and chairs, desks, and a few big soft chairs, too.

"I read about this room," Mother said. "It's called the Writing Room. Isn't it beautiful?"

"Why is there a room just for writing?" Alice asked.

"Oh, in case people want to write letters home. At the first port the ship docks in, they can mail their letters. And some people like to write down what happens on a trip so they won't forget. They write in little notebooks called journals—like a diary."

In several places along the deck they found tables and chairs. Mother and Alice sat down at one of the tables and watched the ocean roll away behind the ship.

They were wandering around deck three when they found the dining room. It was huge. The dining tables and chairs were made of dark, polished wood and had curvy legs and arms. Big arches led into other parts of the dining room. The curved ceiling had interesting designs and paintings on it.

"How lovely," Mother said, in a half-whisper.

They had almost reached their cabin when a boy ran past them.

" 'Scuse me," he said, and slipped into the cabin next door. Number fifteen.

Alice blinked her eyes. She had never seen such bright red hair on anyone. She stayed in the hall for a moment after Mother went into their cabin. Suddenly the door to cabin fifteen opened again, and two heads of flaming red hair poked out of the doorway. The boys looked at her and grinned. Then one of them stuck out his tongue, and they both disappeared back inside.

Alice put her hands on her hips. Her mouth was pressed into a tight line. "Boys!" she muttered.

Later, in the dining room, Alice saw other children, but most of them were closer to Johnny's age.

"There are only babies here," Alice complained. "Nobody my age."

"What about those boys at the table by the window?" Daddy asked.

Alice turned to look. It was the twins from the cabin next door.

"I don't know about them," she said. "Their hair is so red!"

"Since when," Daddy asked, "do you choose your friends by the color of their hair?"

Alice wrinkled her nose. "Yes, but red? I've never seen anyone with hair that bright red before."

Daddy's eyes looked sad. "Are you going to turn up your nose at the Chinese children, too?" he asked. "How would you feel if they wouldn't play with you because your hair is brown and not black?"

Alice looked down at her hands and mumbled, "I'm sorry, Daddy."

The food was served by waiters in white jackets. Alice got a baked potato with a little American flag stuck in the top. She didn't recognize any of the other food—except the chocolate cake at the end of the meal.

"Excuse me, ma'am," one of the wait-ers said with a smile. "Are you Miss Stewart? Miss Alice Stewart?"

No one had ever called her that before. Alice swallowed the last forkful of her cake and glanced at Mother. Then she nodded her head and answered, "Yes, sir," in a small voice.

The waiter bowed and handed her a folded paper. She opened it carefully, her eyes wide with wonder. "Look in the front of lifeboat 6," was all it said.

Alice showed the note to Mother and Daddy.

"Who would send me this note?" she asked.

They all puzzled over it.

"Why don't we go look in the life-boat?" Daddy asked. He wiped Johnny's face and hands and picked him up. "Let's go see what this is about."

On the way out of the dining room, they met the family with the two red-headed boys. The parents introduced themselves. The twins and Alice stared at each other.

The family was named Johnson. They were from Iowa and were on their way to be missionaries in Hong Kong. Alice heard the father call the boys Pete and Andy. She wondered if their mother and daddy could tell them apart.

Daddy explained about Alice's note and asked if the Johnsons knew where lifeboat six was. They didn't.

So Daddy got some directions from a crew member passing by. And finally they found lifeboat six on the open deck at the end of their own hallway. Daddy lifted Alice up so she could reach inside the boat. When he set her down, she held an envelope with her name on it.

Pete and Andy crowded eagerly beside her.

"Open it!" one demanded.

"What's it say?" asked the other.

Alice looked from one to the other. She enjoyed making them wait. Slowly she slipped her thumb under the flap and opened the envelope.

"Hurry up!" the boys urged impatiently.

When she pulled out the paper and unfolded it, they pushed closer to see what it said. Together they read it out loud.

"Go to deck two at ten o'clock tomorrow morning. Find a sailor with a gray beard. Ask him if his name is Mr. Murphy."

"Wow!" said one of the boys. "This is a mystery!"

"Yeah," said the other. "We know where that deck is. We'll take you there tomorrow so you won't get lost."

Alice looked at Daddy for permission. He nodded his head and smiled. "That's a good idea," he said.

"You're in cabin fourteen, right?" asked the first boy. "We'll come get you in the morning, OK?"

For a while the grown-ups sat in the deck chairs and got to know each other. Johnny ran around in circles, singing to himself. Alice and the boys stood on tip-toe to look over the side of the ship. They were hoping to spot some fish.

When they tired of staring at empty, end-less ocean, Alice looked at one of the boys and asked, "How do people tell you apart?"

"It's easy," said one.

"Yeah," said the other.

"But how?" Alice wanted to know.

One of the boys pointed to the other. "See that big freckle on his cheek? That's Andy. I'm Pete. I don't have a big freckle."

"What do you mean?" Alice asked. "You're both covered with freckles."

"Yeah," said Pete. "But not one that big. That's huge!"

"And," Andy added, "Pete's got a scar on his chin. Last year he fell off a brick wall and cut his chin open." Andy grinned. "It was really keen. Blood shot out and squirted all over! He got to go to the hospital for stitches. Four big black ones."

"Andy," scolded his father. "That's enough! Don't make Alice sick."

Soon they all said good night and went to their cabins. Daddy read the story about Jesus in a boat on the Sea of Galilee to Alice while Mother got Johnny ready for bed. Johnny was asleep before she finished buttoning his pajamas.

Daddy pulled Alice onto his lap, and Mother sat down beside them.

"Well, my dear," Mother said, "have you enjoyed your first day aboard ship?"

Alice's eyes sparkled. "Oh, yes! Isn't this ship wonderful?"

"I see you've made some friends, too— in spite of their red hair," Daddy added. "I'm sure you'll have fun with them."

Mother chuckled softly. "And you have a mystery to solve. I think the twins will help you a lot with that."

CHAPTER 2

"And
Be
Ye Alice?"

Daddy rested his head against the high back of the sofa. Alice leaned against his chest. She could hear his heart beating. Mother pulled her feet up and snuggled against the other side of him.

Daddy reached for Mother's hand. "Well," he said, "we're on our way. Only God really knows what's ahead of us. So let's enjoy our time on this ship and consider it a blessing. I have a feeling that the train ride from Hong Kong won't be as comfortable."

Daddy was quiet a moment. Then he said slowly, "And once we get to Shanghai . . . well . . . it won't be like this at all."

Mother reached over and patted Alice's arm. "It feels good to be doing what God wants us to, doesn't it?" she said. Alice nodded, but her eyes were beginning to droop.

"Before you fall asleep," Daddy said, "let's finish our worship with a prayer."

They knelt together and Alice tried to stay awake until Daddy said "amen." After she got ready for bed, Daddy pulled a lever on the sofa. A bed slid out, all made up. Alice curled up under the covers with a smile on her face, ready for her first night on board a ship.

Thank You, Jesus, she thought. *Thank You for this pretty ship, and for my new friends—even if they do have red hair—and . . . and for my mystery! I think it's exciting*

"And Be Ye Alice?"

to be a missionary. And I'll be a good one, Jesus. I promise.

The next morning Johnny woke Alice by crawling up on her bed and sitting on her chest.

"Allie! Allie!" he sang as he bounced up and down.

Alice groaned and rolled over. Johnny tumbled off, giggling. *No use getting mad,* she thought. So she sat up and started tickling him. They laughed and played until the door opened and Daddy walked in.

"You two still in bed?" he said. "I'm hungry! Doesn't anybody want to go to the dining room?"

Mother leaned out of the bathroom door. "I'll be ready in a minute," she said. "I'm just brushing my teeth. Then I'll get Johnny ready. Hurry up and get dressed, Alice."

Daddy picked up Johnny. "I'll start dressing this little wiggle-worm," he said. "It's so beautiful outside. I already walked around the deck five times."

Alice raised her eyebrows. "Why did you do that?"

"For exercise," he said. "We'll do a lot of sitting around and eating aboard ship.

"This afternoon," Daddy continued, "I'm going to write some letters. I need to let Grandma and Grandpa know how we're doing. Maybe I'll write a note to Dr. Adams, too. Do you want to write a letter to Ruth? You can send it in my letter to her father."

"Could I write in that special Writing Room?" Alice asked.

"Certainly. That's where I'll be. The ship provides the paper and envelopes. And maybe even the ink and the pens, too."

After breakfast in the dining room, Alice waited impatiently for Pete and Andy to come.

"And Be Ye Alice?"

"I'm sure you'll be safe if the three of you stay together," Mother told her. "Just remember our cabin number. And don't hang over the side of the ship."

Soon Alice heard two people knocking on their cabin door.

She laughed. "They even knock at the same time," she said, running to open the door. "'Bye, Mother."

The boys led her up the narrow stairway to deck two. It was almost ten o'clock. They stayed close together and walked slowly, looking for a sailor with a gray beard. They finally saw him in the distance. He was dressed all in white. Behind his head, the back of his big square collar flapped in the ocean breeze. The legs of his pants were skinny down past his knees, but wide at the bottom. Alice had heard them called "bell bottoms," and that's just what they looked like—big bells.

The sailor was coiling a rope into a

HIDDEN NOTES AND HIGH SEAS

neat pile on the deck. When he saw the children watching him, he grinned and limped over to them.

"Be ye a-lookin' for Mr. Murphy?" he asked. His voice sounded scratchy, but his blue eyes danced with fun.

Alice couldn't find her voice, but Andy spoke up. "Yes, sir, we are. Are you him?"

"Aye, that I am," he answered. Then he smiled at Alice. "And be ye Alice?"

Pete giggled at the funny way Mr. Murphy talked. Alice nodded.

"Uh," she began. "Uh, do you . . . um, maybe have a note for me, Mr. Murphy?"

"Aye, aye," he said, patting his shirt pockets. He finally pulled out a folded piece of paper. He bowed as he gave it to her. "Here ye be. Now be off with ye."

"Thank you, thank you," all three of them shouted back to Mr. Murphy as they ran to the stairway. They raced down the stairs and didn't stop until they were on the deck at the end of their own hall.

"What does it say?" Pete asked eagerly.

"Open it," Andy urged. "Hurry up!"

Alice spread out the paper on a small table nearby. It read, "After lunch on Sunday, look under your pillow."

CHAPTER 3

Pete
and Andy
and the Sabbath

"Wow!" Pete said in a voice filled with wonder. "Another clue!"

Andy looked at Alice. "You won't look until we're here, will you? You'll wait for us, right?"

"I wish it would be here tomorrow. Why do we have to wait until Sunday?" Andy wanted to know.

"I don't know," Alice replied. "Maybe it's because tomorrow is Sabbath."

"Huh?" Pete looked at her as if she

had gone crazy. "What are you talking about? Tomorrow is Saturday. The Sabbath is the day after."

"No, it's not!" Alice said hotly.

"Hey, take it easy," Andy said. "We're the only kids our age on this ship. We've gotta stick together." He frowned. Then he looked at Alice. "Do you really keep Sabbath on Saturday?"

Alice nodded.

"Do you even go to church on Saturday?" he asked again.

She nodded again.

"How come?" Pete asked.

Alice paused. "Uh, because my parents do . . . and . . ." She added quickly, "Because Jesus did."

"Really?" Andy asked. "I've never heard of anybody going to church on Saturday."

"Weird," was Pete's only comment.

"It's not weird," Alice fired back. "Lots of people do it. And all the Jews do it too! Don't you know the Ten Commandments?"

"Of course we do."

"Well, say the fourth one," she snipped. "It begins 'Remember the Sabbath day to keep it holy.' "

"We know that!" Pete said. "We learned them, too, you know."

Andy looked bewildered. "But we *do* keep the Sabbath," he said. "Every Sunday we go to church—everybody does."

"No, everybody doesn't," Alice replied. "I don't. Neither do any of my friends."

"Aw, forget it," Pete said, changing the subject. "Can we come at one o'clock on Sunday and look under your pillow with you?"

"OK," Alice agreed. "But don't be late—or I'll look without you." As she turned to go, she waved her hand. "See you later."

When Alice got back to her cabin, she showed the note to Mother.

"Look," she said. "I found another note. I wonder who's writing them. Do you think it's that waiter who gave me the first one?"

"Could be," Mother said, looking up from the book she was reading. "Daddy took Johnny for a walk. Why don't you get your book and join me? There's room on this sofa for both of us."

Mother tucked her feet up under her and smiled. Alice dug in her bag and pulled out her own book.

For a few minutes the cabin was quiet. But Alice couldn't keep her attention on the book. Finally she laid it down.

Mother looked up. "What's the matter, dear?"

Alice glanced at the cover of her book for a moment. Then she looked at Mother. "Pete and Andy go to church on Sunday," she said.

"Well, dear, lots of people do."

"Then why do we go to church on Saturday, Mother?"

"You know why," Mother said. "You've learned the Ten Commandments. Remember?"

"Yes, but so have Pete and Andy. They say it's weird to go to church on Saturday."

Just then the door opened and Daddy walked in with Johnny sleeping on his shoulder. After he laid Johnny in the crib, he pulled a chair up in front of the sofa and sat down. He slipped off his shoes and rested his feet on the sofa cushion between Mother and Alice and smiled.

"Well, what are my two favorite ladies talking about so earnestly?" he asked.

"Alice is growing up," Mother said. "At home all her friends were Seventh-day Adventists. Now, she has some new friends—and some new questions."

"Pete says I'm weird, Daddy," Alice

explained. "He and Andy say that Sunday is the Sabbath day."

Daddy smiled. "According to the Bible, Sabbath is the seventh day of each week. And you can just look at a calendar to see which day is the seventh. When Jesus was on earth, He always kept the Sabbath." Daddy shifted in his chair. "And He told His followers to do the same thing."

"But a long time ago," Mother added, "many Christians began keeping Sunday to celebrate the day that Christ woke up and came out of His grave."

"Isn't that important to us too?" Alice asked.

"Very important," Mother replied. "And Adventists do celebrate it—but we do it with baptism. People come up out of the water brand new just like Jesus came out of the tomb."

Daddy leaned forward. "Sunday-keeping Christians love God just as much as we do. They just haven't reached the point yet where they see how important the true Sabbath is."

"So Jesus never went to church on Sunday?" Alice asked.

"Only for special programs—just like we do sometimes. But that doesn't mean we change our Sabbath," Daddy replied.

Alice sat up straight. "And Jesus stayed in the grave on Sabbath! That's important, isn't it?"

Daddy nodded. "That's right. And do you remember what God did on the seventh day of creation?"

"He rested!" Mother and Alice answered at the same time, then laughed together.

Daddy glanced at his watch.

"One more thing," he said, "and then we'll wake up Johnny and go to lunch."

"What's that, Daddy?"

"Don't argue with people about the Sabbath, Alice. We'll never convince people to believe in God's true Sabbath by arguing with them." He stood up. "Now, let's go eat!"

Alice's forehead scrunched up. She thought hard as she followed Mother and Daddy to the dining room. Why not tell Pete and Andy that they were wrong about Sabbath? She'd ask Daddy more about that later.

In the afternoon, Alice walked to the Writing Room with Daddy. She felt very grown up as she sat next to him at a desk. The writing paper had a little drawing of their ship on it. Under it was the ship's name written in fancy letters: SS *President Jefferson*.

She wrote to Ruth about their cabin, and about Pete and Andy. "You wouldn't believe how red their hair is!" she wrote. "And they have a million freckles on their faces." Then she added, "I miss you. I wish you were here. We could have so much fun together on this ship."

Two tears dropped onto the paper. The ink ran in tiny puddles where the tears fell. She wiped her cheeks with the back of her hand. Then she began a note to Grandma and Grandpa. When she handed her letters to Daddy, tears were running down her face. He put his arm around her and gave her a hug.

"I know," he said gently. "Sometimes I feel like crying too. We are excited about doing God's work in China, but we miss our family and our friends so much."

He slipped her letters into the envelopes with his and then licked the flaps and pressed them shut. "Come on," he said, kissing the top of her head. "Let's go get a glass of lemonade."

The Stewarts' first Sabbath on board ship passed quickly. They sang Sabbath songs and prayed together. Then Mother read some Bible stories out loud.

After lunch, Mother put Johnny down for a nap. Alice and Daddy took the Bible storybook to a quiet place on one of the decks. Daddy had just started reading out loud when Pete and Andy walked by. In a moment they turned around and came slowly back. Soon they were sitting cross-legged on the deck listening too. Later, Daddy took all three of them to the back of the boat. At Daddy's suggestion, they all sat in the deck chairs. They scooted down until they were almost lying flat.

"Now," Daddy said, "what can you find in the clouds? I see one that looks like a whale!"

"There's a rabbit!" exclaimed Pete, pointing straight up.

Alice had fun looking for clouds that looked like animals and toys. The time went by as fast as the clouds did.

Just before suppertime, the boys politely thanked Dr. Stewart for the nice afternoon.

Andy looked at Alice and added, "You do fun things on your Sabbath." Then he looked down at his shoes, and back at Alice's daddy.

"Um, sir? Uh . . . can we come spend next Saturday with you? Please?"

Daddy laughed. "Of course you may!" he said. "We'll be glad to have you."

As the boys left, Alice smiled. "Daddy, I think I understand now what you said before."

Daddy chuckled. "What are you talking about, Little Lady?"

"You said I shouldn't argue with Pete and Andy about the Sabbath. I didn't understand why. But now I do," she said.

"What do you mean?" Daddy prodded.

"Well, if I'd argued with Pete and Andy, nothing would have changed. But because you made Sabbath fun for us, they want to spend next Sabbath with us too."

Daddy hugged her. "You'll make a good missionary," he said.

Pete and Andy and the Sabbath

Promptly at one o'clock on Sunday Alice heard two knocks on the door. She ran to open it.

"Have you looked yet?" Pete demanded.

"Nope," Alice replied.

"Well, what're we waiting for?" Andy said. "Where do you sleep?"

"On that sofa," Alice said, pointing to it.

"But—where's your pillow?" Pete asked, looking worried. "The note said to look under your pillow."

"It's on a stack of blankets in the closet." Alice opened the closet door and reached down for her pillow. Pete and Andy crowded close beside her.

As she lifted her pillow, a piece of paper floated down to the floor. Pete snatched it up. Alice took it and opened it slowly.

"Hurry up!" Andy urged.

"You always take too long," Pete whined.

Finally Alice flattened the paper with her hand, and Andy read it out loud.

" 'Show this note to a waiter named Bill at the sandwich counter on deck two. He will give you three ice cream cones.' "

"Wow!" Pete yelled. "Let's go!"

Andy hesitated. "Hey, Alice . . . who's sending you these notes?"

"I don't know." She shrugged her shoulders. "At first I thought it was the waiter in the dining room. But now I don't know."

Pete grew impatient. "Who cares? Let's go get ice cream."

Alice opened the door. "Well, don't just stand there! Come on!"

CHAPTER 4

A Storm at Sea

"Having fun?" Mother asked.

Alice looked up from the game of checkers she was playing with Daddy at a little table on the deck.

"I'm winning!" Alice boasted. "Look at all of Daddy's black pieces I have." She laughed.

Johnny pulled at the table, trying to see what was on it. "Me! Me!" he demanded.

"Not yet, Johnny," Daddy said. He grabbed the table before Johnny pulled it over. "When you get just a little bigger you can play."

"Come along, Johnny," Mother said, reaching for his hand. "Let's finish our walk."

"Wait a minute, Millie," Daddy said. Then he turned to Alice. "You're so far ahead I'm sure you'll win. So how about you take Johnny for his walk? That will give Mother a break for a few minutes."

Alice looked at the game and then at Daddy. "You just don't want to lose," she said, grinning. Finally she agreed. "OK. Come on, Johnny. Let's go."

"By the way," Mother said, sitting down in Alice's chair. "Pete and Andy are outside on deck four. They looked pretty bored. They asked where you were."

Alice headed toward the stairs. "We'll go find them," she said. "Maybe they will give Johnny a horsey ride."

Daddy laughed. "Don't be too hard on the boys," he called after her.

A Storm at Sea

When they reached deck four, Alice spotted Pete and Andy standing on tiptoe, reaching over the side of the ship. They were pretending to fish.

"What are you guys doing?" she asked. "Do you think you're some of Jesus' fishermen-disciples?"

"Yep," Andy spoke first. "That's who we are."

Pete grinned. "We *are* Peter and Andrew, you know."

"For sure?"

"That's us," Pete said.

"Didn't you know?" Andy asked.

"How would I know?" Alice sounded annoyed. "No one ever told me your names were short for Peter and Andrew."

"Well, don't get mad about it," Pete said. "Stop it, Johnny!"

While they were talking, Johnny had been pulling first on Andy's pant leg, then on Pete's.

"Horsey!" Johnny begged. "Ride horsey."

Alice laughed.

Andy gave Pete a push. "Down on your knees, brother."

Pete frowned, but he got down on his hands and knees.

Johnny climbed on—and immediately fell off on the other side. Two more times he tried, but by then they were laughing so hard they all collapsed on the deck. Johnny laughed as hard as the others.

Finally Andy picked Johnny up and commanded the "horsey" to hold still. "OK, Johnny," he said. "Hang on to the horsey's shirt so you won't fall off." He gave Pete a swat on the rear end. "Go, horsey!" he ordered.

Pete took off at a fast trot, and soon Johnny slid off onto the deck again. It became a game for them all.

Pete and Andy took turns giving Johnny rides. Alice shrieked encouragement. They all laughed until their sides ached. Finally Pete and Andy rolled over on the deck and refused to get up.

"Stop!" Andy cried, as Johnny bounced on his tummy. "No more horsey rides today." He sat up and rubbed his knees.

Pete rubbed his, too. "Ow-w-w! That deck's hard," he said. He pulled up his pant legs and looked at his knees. "Gosh, no bruises yet." He sounded disappointed.

"Hey!" Andy said sternly. "You're not supposed to say that word!"

"What word?"

"You're not supposed to say 'gosh,' " Andy told him. "Father says it's just another word for God. So that makes it swearing. And Christian men don't swear—especially in front of ladies."

"OK, OK," Pete replied. "But Alice isn't a lady."

"So what—she's a girl. That makes it worse."

Alice stood with her hands on her hips, glaring from one to the other. "I am too a lady!" she said firmly.

"Hey, look!" Andy exclaimed, pointing toward the sky. The horizon had suddenly grown dark. As Alice looked, she saw a bank of dark gray clouds towering like a wall in front of the ship. Just as the wind caught her skirt, Daddy came running onto the deck.

"Get inside—hurry!" he shouted. Daddy grabbed Johnny and turned quickly. The other three ran after him as the wind began to howl. The ship leaned over toward one side as they entered the cabin. A book Daddy had left on the desk slid to the floor. Alice could hear things falling in their little bathroom—probably the lotion bottles Mother left there.

"Wow!" Pete exclaimed, looking out the little window.

A Storm at Sea

"Let me see, too." Andy pushed him aside.

Alice stood behind them. "What? What is it?"

Andy turned. "Nothing," he said. "Absolutely nothing. It's so black out there you can't see anything."

Alice took a quick look. It wasn't even suppertime, but it was as dark as night outside.

Daddy slipped out the door and returned almost immediately.

"Your folks aren't in your cabin," he said, looking at the boys, "so you'd better stay here with us." Then he looked at Mother.

"Millie?" Daddy spoke with a question in his voice. "You're so pale! Are you getting seasick?"

Mother caught the wall to keep from falling over when the ship rocked again. "I'll be all right," she said, but her voice sounded weak. Alice thought she sounded like a little girl.

Daddy set Johnny on the floor and took Mother's arm. "I think you'd better lie down." He guided her to the bed and insisted she stay there for a while. "After all," he said, trying to tease her, "you have to do as I say. I *am* your doctor, remember?" Mother smiled faintly.

Alice and the boys huddled together on the sofa. Johnny, however, thought it was all fun. He rolled around on the floor, laughing when the ship pitched from one side to the other.

Suddenly there was an urgent knock on the door.

CHAPTER 5

Where's Johnny?

Daddy opened the cabin door.

Mr. and Mrs. Johnson stood there, looking worried. They held on to each other to keep from falling down. Then they both began to speak at once. Their voices sounded worried. "Have you seen—" Mr. Johnson began.

"Oh, thank God!" Mrs. Johnson interrupted.

Daddy grinned. "Yes," he said. "The boys are in here. Come join us." He stepped back just as the ship rolled again. The Johnsons almost fell into the room. "We may as well ride out this storm together, don't you think?" Daddy asked.

Mrs. Johnson wiped her eyes. "We were so afraid that Pete and Andy might have been looking over the side of the ship when the storm hit. That maybe they'd gone overboard."

"Aw, Mom," Andy said. "We were safe the whole time."

"Yeah," Pete added, grinning. "Dr. Stewart came and yelled at us to come in."

Mr. Johnson reached out to shake Daddy's hand. "I'm grateful to you," he said. "Why don't I get a chair or two from our cabin. We may as well all have places to sit."

Soon they were settled down comfortably. Daddy and Mr. and Mrs. Johnson visited quietly.

Where's Johnny?

As Pete, Andy, and Alice listened with wide eyes, Daddy and Mr. Johnson began to talk about other storms. About how Jesus calmed storms. Finally, Mr. Johnson read a few verses from a little Bible he pulled from his pocket, and Daddy prayed.

"Dear Father in heaven," he began. "All of us are going to a foreign country because we know that You want us there. We will serve You with all our strength and intelligence. We want to tell people how much You love them. Please guide our ship safely through this storm. We know that You can stop the storm if You choose. And You can protect our ship. We feel safe in Your hands, Father-God. Help us if our faith becomes weak."

Daddy was still praying when Alice began her own silent prayer. *Jesus, I'm scared. Help me to be brave. And make Mother feel better. And—*

Andy nudged her and hissed, "Get up!"

Daddy's prayer was over, but Alice hadn't noticed. She slipped back onto the sofa. Her face felt hot, and she was glad no one was looking at her. They were distracted by a knock on the door.

It was Philip, their steward. "I'm just trying to find everybody on my hall," he said, looking around. He smiled. "This looks like a party!"

He took a little package of crackers from his pocket. "Anyone seasick here?" he asked. "This may help a bit."

"Thanks," Daddy said, taking them. "I'll take it for my wife."

He held out the crackers to Alice. She jumped up and took them to Mother. Alice had to coax her to eat them.

"One other thing," Philip added, backing out the door. "The dining room will be closed tonight. Too many things are rolling around the floor. And too many people are seasick. So I'll bring around some food that will see you through the evening."

He looked at Mr. Johnson. "Shall I bring the food for your family here also, sir?"

"Certainly," Daddy answered for him. "We plan to spend the evening together."

"Then I'll be right back with both of your picnics," Philip said as he left.

Within fifteen minutes he returned, carrying a box brimming with sandwiches, fruit, and cookies.

"There are bottles of juice and water in the bottom of the box," Philip said. "I'll come back later to take away the trash and see if you need anything else."

Daddy started to lay the food out on the little desk, but the first sandwich he took out skidded across the desktop and landed on the floor. Daddy shrugged his shoulders and set the whole box on the floor.

"Dinner's ready," he said. "Come help yourselves."

Mother appeared in the archway. "May I join you?" she asked. Her voice still sounded a little weak.

"Oh, Mother! Are you better? I prayed for you!"

Mother sank down on the sofa. "Thank you, dear. Yes, I'm a little better. I don't feel well enough to eat yet, but you're having so much fun, I couldn't stay in bed."

Daddy was busy pulling the bottles from the bottom of the box.

"Hey!" he exclaimed. "What's this?" He held up a white paper—the same kind all Alice's notes had been written on.

She jumped up. "Is it for me? What does it say?!"

"Well, let's see who it's addressed to." Daddy stood up, holding the paper out of her reach. He laughed down at her. "Hmmm. All it says is 'To P.A.A.' I wonder who that is."

"Pa? Who's pa?" Pete asked, looking puzzled.

Where's Johnny?

Suddenly, Andy started laughing.

"What's so funny?" Alice demanded.

"Don't you see?" Andy said, still holding his sides. "It's not 'pa.' It's P-A-A. And it stands for Pete, Andy—"

"And Alice!" yelled Alice. "Quick! What does it say?"

Daddy slowly opened the paper. His eyes twinkled merrily. "It says . . ." He paused and looked at them.

"Hurry up, Daddy!" Alice urged. Pete and Andy jumped, trying to reach the paper.

"OK," Daddy said. "Here goes. It says, 'Look under the sofa in the Stewarts' cabin.' "

All three immediately dropped to their knees to look under the sofa.

"Aw, there's nothing there," Pete said, disappointed.

"Daddy, are you sure that's what it says?" Alice asked.

Daddy handed her the paper so she

could see he'd read it correctly.

"Wait a minute," Andy said, his head almost under the sofa. "There's something stuck to the bottom of the sofa. Near the back. I can't quite reach it."

All three tried to reach it. Then they tugged on the sofa to pull it away from the wall.

But a sofa with a bed inside is heavy. They managed to move it only two inches. Finally they looked at their dads.

"Will you help us—please?" Alice pleaded.

"I wonder," Mr. Johnson said as he bent over to move the sofa, "how often God stands and waits to be asked—when He wants to help us so much?"

In a minute, they had slid the sofa away from the wall enough for Andy to pull out the note. "Look for Mr. Murphy on deck 2 tomorrow at 3:30," it read.

"Well, well," Mr. Johnson exclaimed. "So you're still getting notes, are you?

Where's Johnny?

Have you figured out who's sending them?"

"I thought I knew," Alice said. "Now I'm not so sure. Do you think it might be that man who brought the food?"

"Philip?" Daddy asked. "It could be. He has the keys to our cabin."

They talked about the mystery while they finished eating.

"Oh!" Daddy exclaimed. "I just thought of something. You kids may not be able to go up on deck two tomorrow. If it's still storming, you'll have to stay right here."

Suddenly Mother jumped up and looked around, searching. "Where's Johnny? I don't see him!" she said, grabbing the arm of the sofa as the ship rocked. "Do you think he slipped out when Philip brought the food?"

"I didn't see him near the door," Mrs. Johnson said. "But where could he hide in a cabin this small?"

CHAPTER 6

A
Little
Homesickness

They all began searching for Johnny—
in the closet, in the bathroom, behind the
big bed. Then Andy got down on his sore
knees.

"I found him!" he said in a muffled
voice.

"Where?" Mother asked. She couldn't
see Andy.

"Here—under the bed." Andy stood
up. "But I don't know how to get him
out. He's asleep!" They all laughed. It

was a relief to know they hadn't lost Johnny.

Daddy got down beside Andy and gently pulled Johnny out from under the bed. Then he carefully lifted him and laid him in his crib. Mother pulled off his shoes and tucked him in.

"I guess today was just too exciting for Johnny," she said, patting him on the back.

All night long the storm raged and the ship rolled back and forth, up and down. No one talked much. But no one wanted to go to bed, either. Alice fell asleep several times, but each time, she woke up again after a few minutes. She listened to the wind howling and to Daddy and Mr. Johnson talking quietly. Sometimes they were praying.

By morning, the wind began to die down. Then it finally stopped raining. The water grew calm again. The storm was over.

In the afternoon, when Alice and Pete and Andy went to find Mr. Murphy, they overheard him talking to another sailor.

"I guess them missionary folk was a-prayin'. The captain said the storm was supposed to last three days. But it be a-blown over already."

The kids looked at each other and smiled. They remembered the prayers last night.

Mr. Murphy turned and noticed them. "Well, and how be ye?" he asked. "Did ye be a-prayin' this storm away?"

They nodded their heads, but couldn't find their voices.

"I reckon y'r wantin' this here paper I got, right?" he asked.

Again they nodded.

Finally, Alice spoke in a high voice. "Yes, please."

"Well, here ye be." He pulled a folded white paper out of his pocket, just like before. Again they ran down to their own deck before they opened it. "Look behind life preserver 29 on deck 2 after dinner tomorrow night," it said.

The next evening, the three eagerly searched for the life preserver. They expected to find another note. But this time, they found a little bag tied there. Lettering on the bag said, "Open with care."

They took it to a table and opened it carefully. In it they found three big pieces of dark, chewy fudge.

"Oh, boy!" Pete exclaimed. "Fudge! I love fudge." He popped a whole piece into his mouth. "M-m-m-m," he said, rubbing his tummy.

Alice and Andy sat down and nibbled on theirs, making it last as long as they could. Then Mother called Alice to come in.

The days followed one after another. Alice was getting tired of being on the ship—even if she was getting notes and treats. She missed Ruth and Mrs.

Boskowitz . . . and Grandpa and Grandma. And her own room and bed. All the days seemed the same. Except Sabbath, when Daddy read Bible stories to her and Andy and Pete. She couldn't remember how many days they'd been on the ship, but it seemed like forever.

"Mother?" she said one afternoon when she and Mother were alone in the cabin. "When are we going to get there?"

"That storm slowed us down a bit," Mother replied. "But it won't be long now. Just a few more days, I think."

"I heard somebody say something about Japan. Are we going there, too?" Alice asked.

"The ship will dock in Japan so some passengers can get off, but we'll stay on board." Mother stood up and stretched. "God has been good to us, don't you think?" she said. "You have friends to play with. We have a nice cabin. And the food has certainly been wonderful. I rather like the SS *President Jefferson.*"

"Yes, but . . ." Alice stopped a moment. "I wish Ruth were here."

Mother sat down beside her and pulled her close. As she ran a hand through Alice's hair, she said, "We're all a little homesick, I think." Mother swallowed—as though she had a lump in her throat. "But we need to think about what's ahead of us and not be sad."

Just then there was a knock on the door. "Special delivery!" called a voice from the hall.

Mother opened the door. A ship's officer handed her an envelope. He saluted her and abruptly turned away.

Mother looked at the envelope and read the name on it. "'Miss Alice Stewart.'" She held it out. "Alice! It's for you!"

Alice jumped off the sofa and reached for the envelope.

As she stuck her finger under the flap, she said, "Pete and Andy will be mad that I didn't wait 'til they were with me. But I can't wait to see what it says." She took out the note and read it.

" 'Tomorrow go with Peter and Andrew to the gift shop on deck two. Show this note to the lady behind the counter.' "

Alice's eyes sparkled again. "The gift shop? Wow! I wonder what will happen there?" Then she turned to Mother. "Mother, may I—"

"Yes," Mother interrupted, laughing. "You may go find Pete and Andy. Off with you now!"

CHAPTER 7

Saying Goodbye Again

The next morning, Pete, Andy, and Alice stood in a row in front of the counter in the gift shop.

"May I help you?" asked the long-nosed, scary-looking lady who stared down at them.

"Um, yes, ma'am," Andy said. He pointed to Alice. "She has a—a—"

"Here." Alice laid the note on the counter. "Are you the lady we give this to?"

The lady looked at the note. She smiled, her whole face lit up, and she didn't look so scary anymore. "Yes, I am." she said, walking out from behind the counter. "Come with me."

She led them to a corner where hats were on display. All kinds of hats. Straw hats in all colors, felt hats, pointed bamboo hats, and sailor hats.

The lady pointed to the hats and said, "You are each to choose whichever hat you'd like from this rack."

Andy looked at her with his eyebrows raised. "Really?"

"Absolutely," she said, still smiling.

"Wow!" Pete exclaimed. "Look! Here's a hat just like Mr. Murphy's! That's the one I want!"

In the end, they all chose matching sailor hats—just like Mr. Murphy's. The lady helped them each find one just the right size. She laughed when they posed in front of the mirror together.

Saying Goodbye Again

"Wow!" Pete exclaimed again. "This is super!"

"Ma'am?" Alice began. "Who . . . uh . . . who gave us these hats?"

The lady's eyes sparkled. "Oh, that would be telling, wouldn't it?"

Someone else entered the shop then, so she had to leave them. But she called back, "Enjoy your sailor hats!"

The three friends didn't pay much attention to the short stop in Japan. Instead, they sat on the deck and talked about Hong Kong and China, making up stories about what they would do there.

Pete rubbed his hands together and grinned. "Just think, Alice! In Shanghai, you'll probably have to eat all kinds of gross things. Like grasshoppers and beetles and cats and snails and—"

"Stop it!" Alice demanded. "You don't know anything about Shanghai! You're just making everything up. I hope you have to eat live worms and—and pigs' feet!"

Andy got up. "C'mon, you guys. Let's go to Alice's cabin and see if her dad will read us a story or something."

"Hey, Alice," Pete asked as they walked along. "Did you ever find out who sent those notes?"

"Uh-uh."

"For sure?"

"I'd tell you if I knew," Alice exclaimed. "Honest!"

"Well, whoever sent them sure was nice," Andy said, straightening his sailor hat.

Pete frowned. "Sure wish I knew who it was."

Several days later the three stood in the bow of the ship, wearing their sailor hats. Silently, they looked toward Hong Kong. The island looked like the back of a turtle, gradually creeping closer. On their right, China drifted past—big, brown, and solid looking. Strange-looking boats sailed through the ocean near the ship. Some had round roofs that attached to each side, providing shelter for the people inside.

Pete and Alice waved toward some of the boats. A few small children waved back.

Andy was silent for a moment. Then he said, "Do you think people actually live on those boats?"

"Sure they do," Alice answered. "Look! See that lady hanging up the wash on that boat over there?"

Alice, Andy, and Pete had already packed their bags. Now they were spending the last hour together. They knew that when they got off the ship, they'd be going to different places. And they probably wouldn't see each other again.

After a while, Daddy and Mr. Johnson came and stood behind them, watching the city get closer. Then

Daddy said, "Well, it's time for us to go gather our things, Alice." Then he turned to Mr. Johnson and held out his hand.

"It's been a pleasure knowing you," he said as they shook hands. "I wish God's blessing on you and your new work."

"And on you, brother," Mr. Johnson answered. "I hope to meet you again sometime, either here or in heaven." Then he turned. "Come along, boys. It's time to say goodbye to Alice and go help your mother."

Pete, Alice, and Andy stared at each other for a moment.

"Well, 'bye," Alice said finally.

"Yeah, see ya," Andy said.

"Don't eat too many bugs!" Pete added with a grin. Then he turned around and ran off before Alice could reply. Andy followed close behind him, and Mr. Johnson trailed after them.

Saying Goodbye Again

Alice leaned against Daddy and took a deep breath and blinked several times to hold the tears back.

Six hours later, Alice stood on the small balcony of their hotel room. Inside, ceiling fans whirred, blowing a slight breeze around the room. Outside, Alice watched crowds of people below, all in a hurry to go somewhere. Her eyes widened as she watched men push through the shoppers while pulling two-wheeled carts. Some carts had seats where people sat; others were piled high with boxes or big bags. She heard lots of loud voices talking in strange tones. And she smelled strange smells that almost choked her.

"Mother, come look!" she called. "I've never seen so many people before."

"Mother's not here," Daddy said as he joined her. "She went with another missionary lady to buy food for our train trip tomorrow night. My! There *are* a lot of people on the streets. This is quite a city!"

"Are we in China now?"

"Well, yes . . . and no." Daddy scratched his head. "The way I understand it, the British are sort of renting Hong Kong from China. So it *is* part of China, and most of the people who live here are Chinese. But it's also a British colony. Does that make sense?"

"Not really." Alice wrinkled her nose. "How come it smells so bad here?"

Daddy laughed. "Food, spices. You'll get used to it," he said. "I hear Johnny waking up. Shall we go down and explore some of the shops?"

Daddy carried Johnny as he and Alice walked down the street. Alice saw a man tying a wooden cage with a live goose in it to the back of his bicycle. The goose squawked as the man pedaled away.

In a small café, she saw people lift their bowls and drink from them. Others picked up food with chopsticks.

Saying Goodbye Again

"I thought people ate with chopsticks only in fancy Chinese restaurants," Alice said. "Do people really eat with them all the time here? Will I have to?"

"Mother insisted on packing some forks," Daddy replied. "But you'll soon learn to use chopsticks. Even Johnny will—when he quits eating with his fingers."

When they got back to the hotel, Mother was looking through her purchases.

"I hope I got enough food," she said. "My, but I'm tired. I guess I'm not used to doing all the grocery shopping. I miss Mrs. Boskowitz!"

At bedtime that night, Alice lay down on the little cot at the foot of the big bed. She looked up at the ceiling. And as she often did, she pretended Jesus was above, smiling down at her.

Dear Jesus, she prayed. *This is my first night in China. This place doesn't smell very* good. Will I get used to it? Take care of Pete and Andy, please. I miss them. I hope they have fun living in Hong Kong—and I hope they don't get in too much trouble!

Jesus, will I have to eat bugs like Pete said? The food here doesn't look very good. But help me not to complain. Help me to be a good missionary. And, Jesus, do You know who sent me those notes on the ship? It was fun to get them. Be sure that whoever sent them knows I liked them!

I'm really sleepy now, so I'll talk to You tomorrow, OK?

CHAPTER 8

Large Wall, Small Door

By sunset the next evening, the Stewart family were on the train, surrounded by their suitcases. Alice noticed that everyone in their train car was Chinese except for them.

Johnny peered curiously over Daddy's shoulder.

Alice laughed. "Johnny likes to look at people, doesn't he? Shall I take him for a walk?"

"You may, but don't leave this car,

OK?" Mother said. "I want to be able to see you all the time."

Partway down the aisle, Johnny stopped and smiled at a white-haired lady.

"Hi," he said, patting her on the knee with his chubby hand.

The lady smiled back, patted him on the head, and spoke some Chinese words. Alice couldn't understand what she said, but Johnny acted like he did! Soon he waved goodbye, and the lady waved back. He stopped four times before they got to the end of the car. Each time he jabbered happily to someone, patting them and smiling.

Alice looked for a water container like the one on the train in America, but she didn't find one. When they got back to their seats, she asked Mother about it.

Mother put her hand up to her mouth, eyes wide open. "Oh, dear, I didn't warn you! I'm glad you didn't find any water."

Large Wall, Small Door

"You mustn't drink water unless we tell you it's safe," Daddy said. "The germs here are different from the ones in our water at home. Since we aren't used to them, this water will make us sick. Even when we have our own house in Shanghai, we'll keep boiled water in a cold place for drinking."

"Here, Alice," Mother said, digging in one of their bags. "In the meantime, we have these bottles of water the missionaries in Hong Kong gave us."

As the hours dragged on, the bench Alice sat on seemed to get harder and harder. She shifted in her seat, trying to find a soft spot.

Daddy chuckled as he watched her. "You won't find a soft spot on a wooden bench, Little Lady," he said. "Let's pull out our pillows and use them as cushions."

The pillows helped, but not much. The hours dragged by for Alice. Every time the train stopped at a station, people held things up to the windows. Alice watched as passengers handed money out the window. They bought packets that looked like some kind of food, bowls of soup, a quilted jacket, and even a live chicken beating its wings inside a wooden box.

Mother opened a package of rice balls and held one out to Alice. "The missionary made these for us, so at least they're clean. We can't be too careful."

Alice wrinkled her nose at them. "Is that all there is to eat?" she asked.

"You'll eat lots of rice balls in China, so you'd better begin to get used to them. Actually they're rather good. Try one," Mother urged.

Shyly Alice reached out two fingers and took one. It felt sticky. She took a tiny bite. Then another. And another.

"Mother?" Alice asked as she licked her fingers a few minutes later. "May I have another one? They're different—but they're kind of good."

The Stewarts didn't sleep much the next few nights. In fact, by the time the train pulled into the station in Shanghai, Alice was more tired than she ever remembered being in her whole life. *Mother and Daddy must be tired too,* she thought, noticing the dark circles under their eyes.

Only Johnny had slept well. But he slept on people—he didn't have to sit on the hard wooden benches and try to sleep. He didn't even wake up when the chicken squawked during the night.

Alice stood with her face pressed against the window as the train pulled into Shanghai just before dark. She was anxious to see her new home.

"Daddy!" she suddenly cried. "Look! Those people by the station are holding up a sign that says 'John Stewart.' "

Daddy leaned over the pile of luggage on the floor between their seats and looked out the window too.

"Over there." Alice pointed to the left. "See that tall man with the blue shirt?"

The train stopped and Alice started to help Daddy pick up their suitcases. Then she looked around her.

"Daddy? Can't we unload our luggage like those people are? See, they're pushing their suitcases through the windows."

"Smart girl!" Daddy said. "I'll go outside, and you and Mother can hand the bags down to me. Is that OK, Millie?"

Mother nudged him toward the door. "Go on! We'll manage here."

Daddy was reaching up for the first bag when the tall man wearing the blue shirt came up to him.

"John Stewart?" he asked.

"Yes," Daddy answered. "Are you from the Adventist mission?"

Large Wall, Small Door

The man reached out to shake Daddy's hand. "Sure am. Welcome to Shanghai! I'm George Brotton. I take care of the coughs and colds at our little clinic. That's my wife Martha over there still holding the sign." He motioned for her to join them. "Let me help you with your luggage." He reached up and took the suitcase Mother and Alice had lifted to the window sill.

The last thing Mother lifted out the window was Johnny. Daddy laughed as he reached up for his squirming one-year-old. Then Mother and Alice left the train by the door at the end of the car. Daddy introduced them to the Brottons.

"Dr. Miller asked me to apologize for him," Dr. Brotton said. "He wanted to meet your train, but he had an emergency at the hospital."

"The hospital's already open?" Daddy asked.

"It wasn't a medical emergency. A builder decided to ignore the plans and do his own thing," Mr. Brotton explained. "By the way, you're to stay in the hospital guest room tonight. And no, the hospital's not quite finished—but at least the guest room has a door on it! Tomorrow Martha will take you to your new home."

"A guest room sounds like heaven—even if we have to sleep on the floor," Mother said, grabbing Johnny before he climbed back onto the train.

Mrs. Brotton smiled. "We can offer you something better than the floor," she said. "There are real beds in the room. You must be exhausted." She turned to her husband. "I think we'd better get this family to the hospital soon. They look about ready to fall asleep standing up."

The Brottons helped carry the Stewarts' luggage as they pushed through the crowd. Out on the street,

Large Wall, Small Door

Alice saw an amazing sight. A Chinese man in a straw hat and shorts sat behind the steering wheel of a truck—at least she thought it was a truck. It had a motor and a place in back to pile suitcases. The motor was running roughly and shook the whole truck. Alice worried it might fall apart if the man actually drove it.

She was surprised to see Dr. Brotton walk over and put the bags he was carrying on the back of the truck. He motioned for the others to do the same.

"Now," he said, "we part company. We men will ride on the back of the truck to protect your things. Martha will take the rest of you in a rickshaw. We'll meet you at the hospital. It's not far."

He stepped into the street to stop a man who was pulling a small bench on wheels. It looked just like the ones Alice had seen in Hong Kong. A long pole was attached to each side of the bench. The man stood between the poles and waited for Mrs. Brotton and Mother to squeeze onto the bench.

Daddy reached for Johnny. "I'll take this wiggle-worm on the truck with me," he said.

Alice sat on Mother's lap, and the man picked up the poles and began to run. He pulled them along the busy street. At first Alice looked around eagerly, trying to take in all the strange sights. She tried to imagine what her new home would look like. Within a few minutes, however, her eyes began to close, and she sank back against Mother.

She woke up in a strange room. Sunshine streamed through the window. Mother was dressing Johnny. Daddy was gone.

"Good morning, sleepyhead! Hurry and get dressed. Daddy went to see the hospital. When he gets back, Mrs. Brotton will take us to the hospital kitchen for breakfast."

Large Wall, Small Door

Alice's eyes sparkled. "Oh, Mother! Isn't it exciting? Today we get to see our house! Do you think I'll have a room of my own?" She smiled as she imagined it. "Maybe it will have white walls and a big window, and lots of shelves for my toys and books."

"Don't get your hopes up too high, my dear," Mother said. "Remember, this isn't Portland. This is China. We'll make the best of whatever we get, won't we?"

Alice was soon ready to go. She gobbled down her breakfast, then waited eagerly for Mother and Mrs. Brotton to finish eating. Finally, the guard at the hospital gate got two rickshaws for them. The hospital yard-keepers had already left with the Stewarts' suitcases.

Today is a special day, Alice said to herself as she rode along. *We are real missionaries now. I am going to help Mother teach people how to be clean and healthy. I'm going to tell Chinese children stories about*

Jesus. But first, I get to see our new home. It will be beautiful. I'm sure it will be.

About fifteen minutes later, the rickshaws stopped beside an ugly concrete wall. Weeds grew from cracks along the edges. Chipped white paint still showed in spots. The only way through the wall was a small door with the paint worn off.

"Why are we stopping here?" Alice asked. "What's this?"

Daddy held out his hand and helped her out of the rickshaw. Then he squeezed her hand a moment longer. "Be brave, Little Missionary," he said. "I think this . . ." He took a deep breath. "This is our new home."

CHAPTER 9

A Strange New World

The door creaked as Mrs. Brotton unlocked it and pushed it open. "Welcome to your new home," she said. "It should be a nice, cozy place, once you're all settled in."

Daddy ducked his head to follow Mrs. Brotton through the low door. Alice and Mother followed. Mother held Johnny's hand tightly.

A deep shelf ran almost the width of the room they entered. A small window peeked above the shelf, right over a little sink. Pots and pans of all sizes hung from the walls. Extra-long chopsticks stuck out of a jar. At the end of the shelf was another door.

Mrs. Brotton was speaking. "This is where your amah will prepare your meals."

"My ah—what?" Mother asked, looking puzzled.

"Amah. Helper," Mrs. Brotton explained, smiling. "Amahs are wonderful women who cook and clean and look after children. Your amah will do whatever you need help with. And your food will cost a lot less if she does the shopping for you."

She paused a moment. "Dr. Miller's wife has already hired an amah to work for you. I hope you don't mind," she said. "Mrs. Miller will bring her over tomorrow morning. Until then, there's food in this cupboard down here. That should tide you over.

A Strange New World

"Oh, and by the way," she continued, "this door we came in is the only entrance into this house, so you should be safe enough."

She led the way out the other door into what Alice guessed must be their yard.

On the left she saw a flat-roofed building with five doors. Beside each door was a window. She peeked into the window by the first door. "Mother! Look at the huge dining-room table! And it has . . . eight, nine, ten—ten chairs around it."

Mother laughed when she saw it. "I guess we'll *have* to have an amah. That table is made for company dinners."

Mrs. Brotton laughed too. "And that's also where you'll have your Chinese lessons," she said. "Your teacher will come here to your home twice a week. He'll begin next Monday, I think."

"Mother already speaks Chinese," Alice told Mrs. Brotton proudly.

"Oh, no!" Mother shook her head. "I learned a little from a teacher in Portland, but only a very little."

Alice opened the door into the next room. The dark wood chairs had carved arms and straight, carved backs. Thin pads covered the seats. There were two sofalike things that looked just like the chairs—only wider. Four people could sit side by side on one. *This living room doesn't look very comfortable,* she thought.

The next room was empty. Only a desk and chair stood in the fourth room. And the last room was the bedroom. It held a huge bed with big, thick, wooden legs. The Stewarts' suitcases lay in a pile beside the bed.

"In China," Mrs. Brotton explained as she led the way into the bedroom, "most families sleep together—all in the same bed. As Americans, you'll probably want to make other arrangements for your children."

A Strange New World

"Mother," Alice whispered in Mother's ear. "Where's the bathroom?"

"I don't know yet," Mother whispered back. "I hope there is one."

Back outside, Daddy looked around. "Well," he said, "you won't have to learn to grow vegetables, Millie. Concrete walls and a concrete yard. Our own private courtyard." He smiled, but Alice thought his chuckle sounded a little disappointed.

"But look!" Mother exclaimed. "Those three big pots of flowers are beautiful!"

"Mrs. Miller planted those flowers for you," Mrs. Brotton said.

"How thoughtful," Mother said. "I must remember to thank her when she comes tomorrow. They really brighten up this old courtyard."

Stairs led to the flat kitchen roof. Mrs. Brotton explained that the amah would hang their washing up there.

Then she pointed straight ahead.

"And there," Mrs. Brotton said, "is an important building." Alice saw a tiny building—only as wide as its two doors.

"That first little room is a shower. It's not like the ones back home in America, but we do the best we can here," Mrs. Brotton explained. "You're lucky. This house has running water in the kitchen and in this little building, thanks to the last Americans who lived here. Otherwise you'd have to dip the water out of a bucket."

"Cold shower, I take it," Daddy said. "What happens in the winter?"

Mrs. Brotton grinned. "You'll figure out something, I'm sure. Oh, and the other little room is the toilet—Asian, not American."

Alice pushed open the door and gasped. "Daddy!" she called. "Somebody stole the—the seat!"

Mrs. Brotton burst out laughing. "Bless the child!" she cried. "This isn't

A Strange New World

America. That hole in the floor *is* the toilet. It works quite well when you get used to it. When you finish, just remember to pull the chain that comes out of the box up on the wall above."

A bell clanged in the kitchen. Someone had pulled the rope on the wall outside. Daddy went to see who had come. It was Dr. Brotton.

"Are you ready to go, Martha?" he asked his wife. "I don't want you going back by yourself."

Then Dr. Brotton looked around. Turning to the Stewarts, he said, "Well, what do you think of your new home? It's not exactly a mansion, is it?"

Daddy and Mother looked at each other and then Daddy answered. "We'll get used to it, I'm sure. Just give us a little time."

When the Brottons left, Mother leaned her head against Daddy's chest. "Oh, John," she said. "How can we make a home out of this old pile of rocks and cement?"

"We'll manage, Millie. With the Lord's help, we'll manage."

Finally, she straightened up and tried to smile. "Let's start unpacking, shall we? Come help us, Alice. We'll leave the doors open so I can keep an eye on Johnny."

Johnny was sitting by one of the big flowerpots, happily playing with a small pile of stones he'd dug out of a flowerpot.

For their first night, they made beds on the floor for Johnny and Alice out of the pads from the living-room furniture. Mother took out a photograph of Grandma and Grandpa Stewart from the bottom of her suitcase and set it on the chest that stood along the wall.

Turning to Daddy, she put her hands on her hips.

"John," she said, "you're going to have to get someone to make a hole in that wall as soon as possible. I want a doorway into the next room. That will be Alice's room. We can get a bed for Johnny in here. But I won't have either of my children in a room that I have to go outside to get to."

"I'm sure it can be done," he said. "I'll check on it at the hospital tomorrow. I think the mission owns this building."

Alice smiled as she set her doll Sally on her sleeping pad. She would have a room of her own again soon. *Thank You, Jesus*, she whispered.

Suddenly, Alice became very still. She stared at the small, white, folded paper on her pillow. It looked just like the notes she had gotten on the ship! How could this be? Slowly, she reached out her hand. It felt like the same paper. Her name was written on the front in the same way. She looked up to see Daddy and Mother watching her. They were smiling.

Carefully Alice unfolded the note. Then she read it out loud. " 'Welcome to your new home in Shanghai. Thank you for being so helpful with Johnny on board the ship. I love you, Little Missionary. Daddy.' "

"Daddy?" she asked just above a whisper. "It was you? It was you all along? And I never guessed!"

She jumped up and ran to give him a big hug. He lifted her off the ground and swung her around. Soon all three of them were hugging and laughing.

"Me! Me!" said a shrill voice from the doorway. Johnny ran over and hugged all the legs he could get his little arms around. Daddy picked him up and hugged him too.

That evening Daddy read a story about Moses for worship. Moses was raised in a king's palace. When Moses grew up, God led him into the wilderness to learn to depend on Him.

A Strange New World

"And God has brought us to Shanghai," Daddy said. "Not exactly a wilderness—"

"But," interrupted Alice, "we will learn to depend on God."

Daddy hugged her. "You're exactly right," he said. "Now, let's pray."

They knelt down in a little circle, and Daddy asked God to teach them to depend on Him more. And to help them make this strange house become a real home for them.

Later Alice and Daddy sat cross-legged on the big bed, talking. Mother was getting Johnny ready for bed.

"Tomorrow," Daddy said, "you might want to write to Ruth and tell her about this odd house. I think Mother brought some paper you can use."

"How can I explain this house to Ruth?" Alice asked. "She won't believe me. Oh—I know! I can draw a picture of it. That will really surprise her. Being a missionary is sure different than I thought it would be."

Daddy laughed. "Wait until you've actually started," he said. "I understand the health class that you'll be helping Mother with has already been announced. It's scheduled to start in two weeks. And soon you'll meet other children at Sabbath School, and learn to speak Chinese, and—"

"Stop, John!" Mother said. "Do you want to scare her?"

"I'm not scared, Mother," Alice said, "just sleepy. If I'm going to do all the things Daddy said, I'd better get some rest!"

She slid off the big bed and snuggled under the thin blanket covering her bed on the floor in the corner. Then she closed her eyes.

I'm here, dear Jesus, she prayed quietly. *I know I told Mother and Daddy I wasn't scared. But I am, sort of. Did I tell a lie? I just didn't want them to know, 'cause they'd worry.*

Can I really help You here? Will You help me learn to talk with those funny-sounding words? Mother says kids learn quickly. I hope I do. And, Jesus, wasn't it fun to learn that Daddy sent all those notes on the ship? I was really surprised!

I'm pretty tired now. But I just wanted to tell You that I'll be a good missionary for You. Please help me learn to like this strange house, OK?

Oh—and one more thing, Jesus—What did Mrs. Brotton mean when she said we'd be "safe enough" here?

If you liked meeting Alice, you've got to meet Sarah, Elizabeth, and Heather—the other Adventist girls!

Sarah, An Adventist Girl (Set 1)

By *Jean Boonstra*. These stories are about a young pioneer girl named Sarah Barnes living in the days of William Miller between 1842 and 1844. This four-book series will entertain and educate children about their Adventist heritage and hope. Titles are: 1. *A Song for Grandfather*; 2. *Miss Button and the School Board*; 3. *A secret in the Family*; 4. *Sarah's Disappointment*.

0-8163-1907-3. Paperback. US$24.99, Can$37.49 set.

Elizabeth, An Adventist Girl, (Set 2)

By *Kay D. Rizzo*. One day, two mystery guests from Maine arrive at Elizabeth's house. The woman, Mrs. White, has visions from God. Big changes happen in Elizabeth's family. Titles are: 1. *The Not-So-Secret Mission*; 2. *Old Friends and New*; 3. *Bells and Whistles*; 4. *Wagon Train West*.

4-33300311-3. Paperback. US$24.99, Can$37.49 set.

Heather, An Adventist Girl (Set 3)

By *Jean Boonstra*. The year is 1898. Heather Gibson can hardly believe her family is moving to Australia. This was the time when Ellen White lived there and wrote her beautiful books on the life of Christ. Meet the new friends and visit the amazing places that become part of Heather's world, in these fun-to-read stories. Titles are: 1. *Secrets and Friends*; 2. *A New Life Down Under*; 3. *A Wedding in Avondale*; 4. *Going Home*.

4-3330-0336-6. Paperback. US$24.99, Can$37.49 set.

Each episode in the Adventist Girl historical series will entertain and educate children about the Adventist heritage and hope.

Order from your ABC by calling **1-800-765-6955**, or get online and shop our virtual store at **www.AdventistBookCenter.com**.

- Read a chapter from your favorite book
- Order online
- Sign up for email notices on new products